BOOK CLUB EDITION

WALT DISNEY'S

The Penguin that Hated the Cold

adapted by Barbara Brenner

BOOK CLUB EDITION

Random House New York

 Published in the United States by Random House, Inc., New York, and simultaneously in Canada by Random House of Canada Limited, Toronto.

Library of Congress Cataloging in Publication Data

Brenner, Barbara. Walt Disney's The penguin that hated the cold.
(Disney's wonderful world of reading)

SUMMARY: Tired of always being cold, Pablo, a penguin, decides to move from the South Pole to a warmer climate.
[1. Penguins—Stories] I. The cold-blooded penguin. [Motion picture] II. Title.
III. Title: The penguin that hated the cold.
PZ10.3.B753Wal [E] 72-12600 ISBN 0-394-92628-5 (lib. ed.)
ISBN 0-394-82628-0

First Edition

Manufactured in the United States of America

J K R

7 8 9

Once there was a penguin named Pablo.
He lived on a block of ice
far away at the South Pole.
The weather there was always cold.

Penguins like the cold.
Most penguins, that is.
But not Pablo.

Penguins like to dive and swim
and catch fish in the icy water.
But not Pablo.

Pablo was the only penguin
on his block who hated cold.

All the other penguins went skiing

and ice-skating.

Or they played all day
in the snow at the beach.

But not Pablo.

Pablo stayed inside, close to the hot stove.
He kept his flippers warm and his feathers warm.

"Cold weather," said Pablo,
"is for the birds.
The other birds. Not me."

One day Pablo said to himself,
"It is silly to be chilly.
I will go where I can
be warm *all* the time."
He put on his skis
and packed his stove on his back.

“So long, you birds,”
he said to the other penguins.
“Wish me luck!”

Oh-oh! Something was wrong.
The stove was pulling him backward.

Pablo was going the wrong way.
Down the hill he went . . . faster and faster.
He was sliding straight toward a cliff.

Suddenly Pablo was hanging upside down. His skis had caught on the icy cliffs.

"Now that was not such a good idea," said the other penguins.

Poor Pablo was frozen stiff.
They had to carry him home to his igloo.

There they held him under a hot shower
until he could walk again.

The next day Pablo had another idea.
He put hot water bags on his feet and under his coat.
He put them around his neck.

"So long, you birds," said Pablo.
"This time nothing can go wrong."

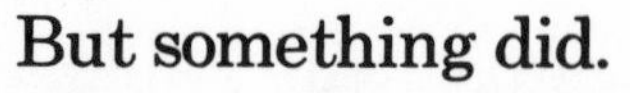

But something did.
When Pablo stopped to look at his map,
the hot water bags melted the snow.
They melted the ice.
Pablo sank . . .

and sank . . .

and sank . . .

down into the ice-cold water.

"Poor Pablo," said the other penguins. "He will never get anywhere."

When they pulled him out,
he was frozen in a block of ice.
And that was the way
they carried him home.

But Pablo's hot stove soon melted the ice.

Next day Pablo said,
"Now I have an idea that will really work.
I will go by boat."

He got a saw and cut a boat
out of the ice under his igloo.

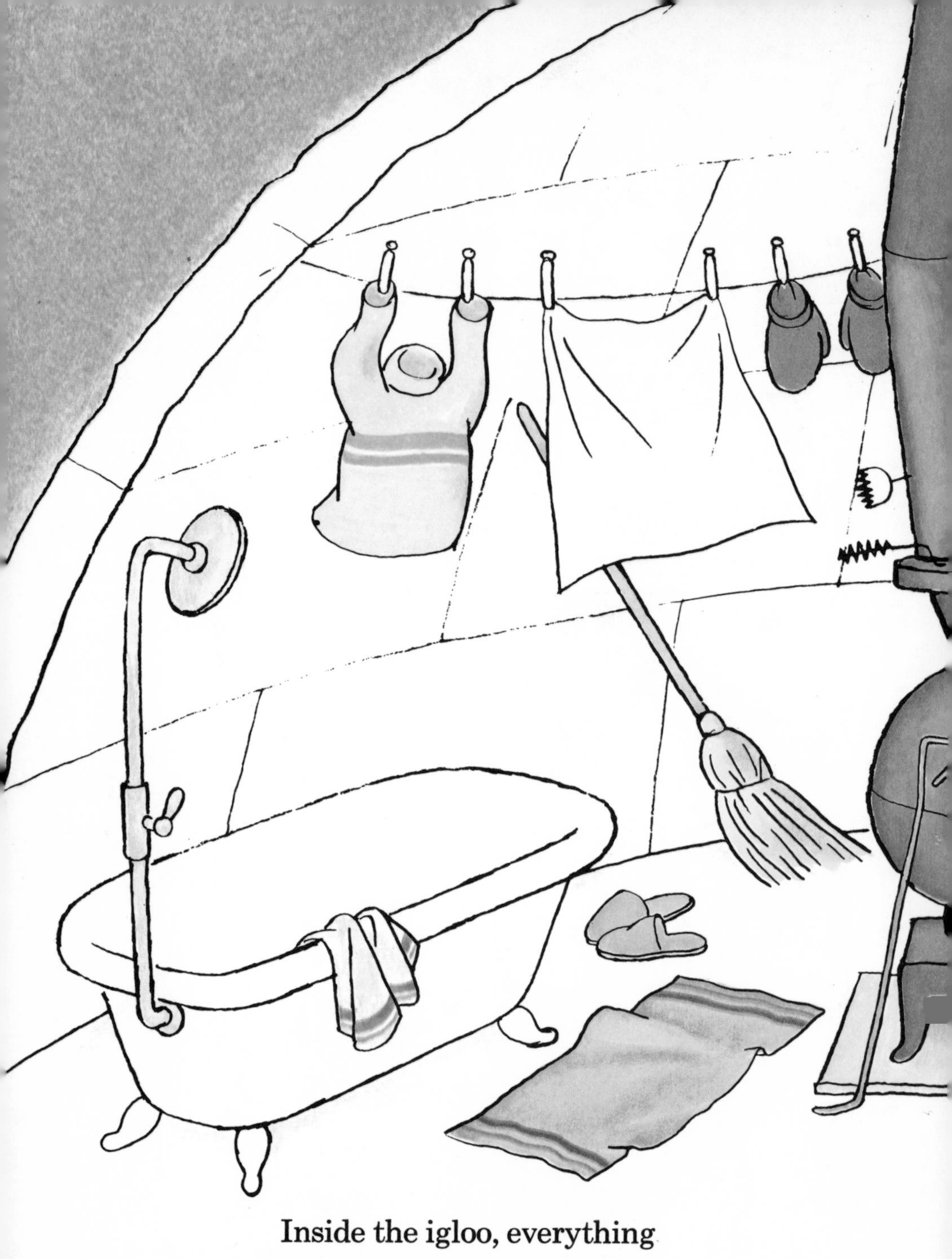

Inside the igloo, everything
was ready for the big trip.

His stove was in place.
His tub was in place.
He was all set to go.

All the penguins on the block came to say good-by. Then Pablo pulled up his sail and off he went.

His boat sailed on and on . . .
. . . through snow and fog . . .

past mountains of ice.

Day after day . . . night after night . . .

Pablo sailed on.

Then one morning
he woke up to find
that the sun was shining.
Hot weather at last!

"I made it!" cried Pablo.

He took off his warm clothes.

He lay down in the warm sunshine.
"Oh, boy," Pablo said.
"This is the life."

But Pablo spoke too soon.
The hot sun started to melt his house.

Then it began to melt his boat.

Soon Pablo was floating on a little piece of ice.
He jumped into the tub.

But there was a hole in the bottom of the tub. Water began to run in.

Pablo had to pour it out as fast as he could.

Quickly he put the shower pipe into the hole.

The water began to splash out of the shower.

Suddenly the tub started to go full speed ahead.

Far away Pablo saw land and trees.

He walked over to a banana tree
and picked a nice yellow banana.

“This looks like a good place to build my house,” he said.

He collected lots of branches

and started building it.

At last Pablo had found the land of his dreams.

No more cold for him!